Where Am I Sleeping Tonight?

A Story of Divorce

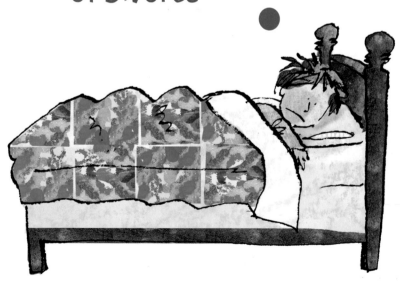

Boulden Publishing
P.O. Box 1186
Weaverville, CA 96093
www.bouldenpublishing.com

Manufactured in China

ISBN-10: 1-878076-30-2
ISBN-13: 978-1-878076-30-4

10 9 8 7 6 5 4 3 2 1

Boulden publishing

Helping you help kids.

Dedication

I dedicate my first book to those people whose love I count on: My mom and dad, who are my role models for being humble, and my daughter, Dara, and husband Mark, who keep me humble.

To my father-in-law Sam, whose memory is a blessing.

To my sister Irene, and her family (Ron, Madison, and Ryden) who always want to hear my stories.

To Angelo Panteli, the principal who first hired me to do what I love — teach, and to Ken Harrison, who gave me the opportunity to bring my new love, writing for children, to fruition.

And to the many children I taught over the years who reciprocated my love and helped me with my stories.

— CGE

To my sister Lainie, who has counseled and helped so many.

— SR

Where Am I Sleeping Tonight?

A Story of Divorce

Carol Gordon Ekster

Illustrated by Sue Ramá

Boulden
publishing

"Mark, whose house are we at?" my little brother Evan whispers.

1

My eyes aren't open, but I am awake. I smell coffee and hear Matty in the Morning's radio show coming from down the hall.

"We're at Dad's," I answer.

Mom and Dad got divorced three years ago. It can be tricky living at two houses. This is our second night at Dad's, and then we'll have two nights at Mom's, then back to Dad's again.

Now that I'm in fourth grade, it's getting complicated. I have a lot to

remember. Like today, my book report

is due. Luckily, it's done and ready to go by the door. But sometimes I forget things. Like I leave a book that I need for homework at Mom's, and Dad has to get it. Or I leave my homework on the counter at Mom's, and she drops it off at school.

Mrs. DeMott, my teacher, feels pretty strongly about how many homeworks I forget.

"Fired! Fired! Fired!

That's what I'd say if you worked for me, Mark. It's important to be responsible."

I've gotten that lecture more times than the

number of pizza nights we have

at Dad's...not that I ever mind

eating pizza.

Evan doesn't have my

problem. I mean, sometimes

he forgets his sneakers for

Phys Ed. He's only in first

grade, and how much

homework does

a first grader get anyway?

Evan and I are dressed, our

teeth brushed, and we

are ready to head out.

Our lunches and book

bags wait for

us at the front

door. This is

our new routine

since Mrs. DeMott left messages on both my parents' answering machines.

Mom replayed it for me, and Dad reported, "Mrs. DeMott is not happy about how many homeworks you've forgotten." He skipped the "I need your cooperation for Mark to succeed." I only forgot one assignment since. (Okay, so it's only been two weeks.) But my mind is made up. I set a goal to be more responsible. Mrs. DeMott is big on goals, and she's a pretty cool teacher.

Dad has his coffee-breath kiss ready for us. When we're at Dad's, it's always a "breakfast at school day". So we just head right out to the bus stop.

"See you guys Thursday. I'll pick you up at school. It's the first day of floor hockey, right?"

I answer, "Think so, Dad." Actually, I feel like saying, "Isn't that what I count on you for, Dad, to help keep my schedule straight? You're the one who got the divorce!"

But my lips stay sealed, tighter than a zipped-up baggy. Evan and I both agree that we like the days at

Dad's better. He wins that contest,

hands down, but we'd never let

Mom know.

It isn't a love contest. It's

about where we can do what we
want. At Dad's we play games until
we're in a computer stupor.

At Mom's, she and our step-dad
have rules, lots of rules. There's no
TV on a test night. (It's not like I
study the whole time anyway!) And
I get only an hour a day of computer
time. After 59 minutes and 59
seconds, Mom calls, "Mark, your

hour is up." It's like she has a timer

in her brain.

I heard Dad on the phone with Mom last night. "Yes, Susan. His book report is propped up by the door, too big to miss."

Both my parents like to make sure I'm not goofing off in school. Last night I thought about picking up the receiver. "Mom, it would be easier to check up on me if you stayed married to Dad!" But I acted like a robot with a computer chip

that demanded, "Resume normal

functioning."

Evan sits next to me on the bus.
He whistles away like a wind-up toy.
He is too young to understand this
whole shared custody thing. Too
young to get confused, or lose track
of reports left on tables at Mom's
house, or under the desk in our room
at Dad's. He is lucky to have me as a
big brother, to help him keep it
all together.

Hmm.
Keep it all together?

I picture Mrs. DeMott's reminder

board right near the door of the

classroom. You'd have to have both

eyes closed to miss it. What if I put one of those wipe-off slates by the door of each house? Evan and I could make checking off the list, part of what we do every morning, no matter which house we're at. Mrs. DeMott would approve. The class has heard all about the importance of making lists and being organized since the first day of school. I couldn't wait to talk to Mom and Dad about this.

Mom and Dad. Every time I

think about how I have to speak to

them separately, I get that bad taste

kind of feeling like when I eat cheese sharp enough to make my whole face pucker. Every wish I've made, on a wishbone or birthday candles, has been a wish for them to get back together. Maybe it's time to wish for something I can actually get.

I decide that for Evan's sake I would point out how lucky we are. We are loved a lot in not just one, but two homes. (Could it be that Mom

and Dad's talks about this have slowly seeped into my brain?)

The bus rolls into its spot near the school, and I slide my arm along Evan's shoulder. He gives me that look like I'm a ten-headed monster with one eye. Can't a guy give his brother a hug? I mean, he is the only other person in the whole world that does this crazy schedule with me. And even if he doesn't get it all yet,

when he starts to have questions, I'll be his answer man. I'll be there for him, every day of the week.

I jump off the bus knowing I have this goal all tied up. It won't just be Evan who can count on me. I run to the playground hearing in my head Mrs. DeMott's new chant when I hand her my homework, "Hired! Hired! Hired!"

And that sounds great to me!